Christmas 1997

Paige —
 This is a beautiful story about the
beauty of your own spirit. You are a very
special little girl on your way to becoming
a very special young women.
 I love you very much...
                    Auntie Chris

"And when your children's children shall think themselves alone in the fields, the store, the shops, upon the highway, or in the silence of the pathless woods, they will not be alone."

CHIEF SEATTLE
1855

DREAMBIRDS

By David Ogden

Illustrations by Jody Bergsma

Little Natsama loved to visit his grandmother, Holima, the medicine woman. On his seventh birthday, Holima told him about dreambirds. "At the beginning and ending of every day, dreambirds spread their wings. One wing reaches out to the sun, and the other reaches out to the moon. Whoever finds a dreambird receives a great gift."

"Grandmother, have you ever found a dreambird?"

Holima smiled, deepening the creases around her moon-pale eyes. She said nothing.

"I think you have, Grandmother. What was your gift?"

"The dreambird's gift is something you must discover for yourself," Holima replied.

"I will become a great hunter!" exclaimed Natsama. "Then I can find a dreambird and claim my gift."

3

Under Holima's guidance, Natsama learned the ways of nature and how to live in the wild. She took him on long treks to gather herbs and other plants used for healing.

One day, while walking through a woodland, they heard leaves rustling in the breeze and ravens cawing in the distance.

"You are learning to recognize the many sounds of nature," said the medicine woman. "But do you know the difference between hearing and

listening?"

When the puzzled boy remained silent, Holima placed her hand over his heart. "You hear with your ears," she whispered, "but you listen with your heart. By listening closely, you can feel your oneness with the source of all things."

Natsama was curious. "Grandmother, what is the source of all things?"

"The source of all things is like a circle," Holima explained. "It is where everything begins and everything returns."

The seasons came and went, but Natsama never forgot his grandmother's story about dreambirds. Determined to find a dreambird and claim his gift, he sought out the best hunters in his village, who taught him the ways of hunting and fishing.

Even his teachers were astounded at how quickly Natsama mastered the skills of the hunter. As word of his prowess spread among the coastal tribes, the strong, young brave became very proud of his reputation. Eventually he believed that no one was his equal, not even Holima, the medicine woman.

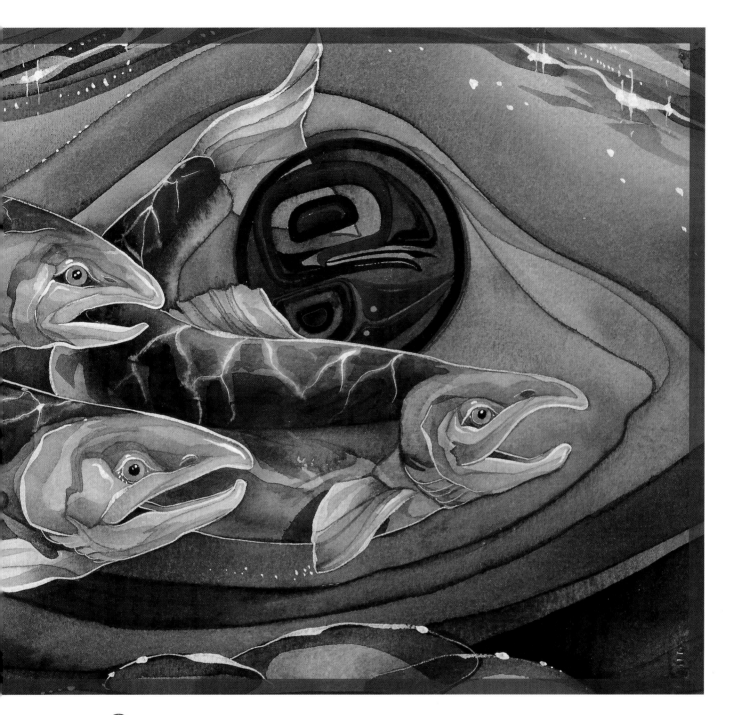

On the evening before his sixteenth birthday, Natsama entered his grandmother's lodge. Standing with his feet planted wide apart, he looked down at the medicine woman and declared, "I am ready to find a dreambird."

"Grandson, have you considered that you may fail?"

"I will not fail!" Natsama exclaimed. "I am the greatest hunter in our tribe."

"Listen carefully," she cautioned, "when you track a dreambird, you must allow it to find you. This requires patience and humility. It will not be easy for such a proud hunter."

"Grandmother, I have earned the right to be proud. I will soon find a dreambird and claim my gift. You will see."

7

Day after day Natsama searched for a dreambird. He saw many birds —
hawks, owls, herons and even an eagle — but he did not find a dreambird.
Reluctantly, the disheartened young hunter returned to Holima's lodge.

Taking his usual place across the fire from his grandmother, Natsama
stared at the rising flames. Finally he said, "Grandmother, I have searched
everywhere without finding even a trace of a dreambird.

"Now I wonder if dreambirds are real. Have I made a fool of myself looking for something that doesn't exist?"

As Holima added cedar boughs to the fire, the crackling of burning embers filled the silence. "Natsama," she said solemnly, "most people never see a dreambird. You must go to the high places and seek the great eagle. In its flight is a sign. Recognize that sign and you will know the secret of finding the dreambird."

Natsama had just left Holima's lodge when two tribesmen paddled by in a canoe. "The medicine woman is having fun with you," they laughed. "We told you there is no such thing as a dreambird. You should have listened." Once his admiring friends, they now openly joked about Natsama — the great hunter of imaginary birds.

Stung by their taunts, Natsama stalked off toward the mountains. For days he searched, but saw only one eagle flying far off in the distance. Again the impatient youth questioned himself, "What could be so important about an eagle's flight? Maybe the others are right and there are no dreambirds."

One cold morning at sunrise, Natsama sighted a majestic bald eagle circling high overhead. In desperation, he pleaded to the soaring bird, "How much failure must I endure? When will you reveal the secret in your flight?"

Without warning, the eagle suddenly plunged toward the earth and disappeared into a deep ravine. As he watched, Natsama felt that he, too, was falling — falling within himself. He remembered being a young boy, curled up beside Holima's fire as she sang his favorite song:

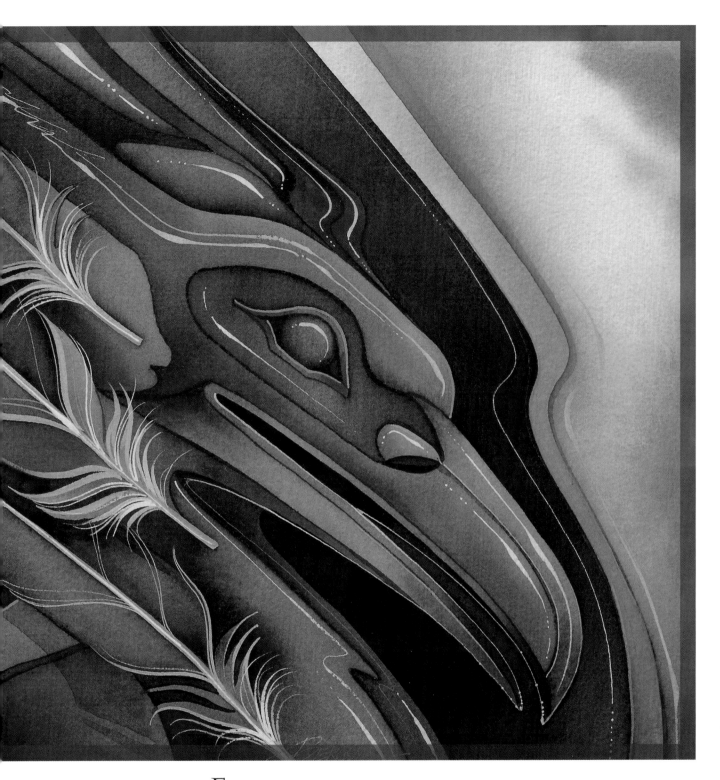

Fish are at home in the water.
Birds are at home in the air.
People are at home on the land.
But there is another home,
Where mysteries once hidden,
Now are revealed.
It is the place within,
The source of all things.

"Now I know where to find a dreambird!" Natsama shouted.

That night Natsama dreamed about the fire in Holima's lodge. Suddenly the flames changed into a glowing, luminous bird that towered over him. On the bird's breast feathers were faint images resembling other hunters from the village. But one image was clear and distinct. It was his own face. "This feather must be the dreambird's gift. I will take it to show everyone that I am still the best hunter." When he reached out to pluck the feather, Natsama awoke.

Early the following morning, he hurried to Holima's lodge. "Grandmother! Last night I found a dreambird."

As Natsama proudly described his dream, the medicine woman listened, occasionally nodding her head. The firelight made her long, silver hair appear to glow.

After the excited youth had finished, Holima paused before replying. "Yes, Eagle has shown that you must go inside yourself to find the dreambird. But last night your pride was dreaming its dream. What you saw was not a dreambird, nor have you received its gift."

Angered by his grandmother's response, Natsama stormed out into the morning mist.

That night Natsama slept fitfully, wondering if he would ever find the elusive dreambird. Just before dawn, he dreamed again of Holima stirring her fire. The embers sparked and hissed, then flared brilliantly. From the swirling flames a silver bird slowly emerged.

16

In the glowing bird's moon-pale eyes, Natsama saw an image of himself. Then the image changed into a small, golden bird that was hopping wildly about. Cocking its head from side to side, it seemed confused and bewildered.

Natsama awoke with a start as a wolf howled in the distance. Shivering in the morning air, he pulled the blanket around his shoulders and recalled his dream. "The silver bird was the same color as Holima's hair. Its eyes were like Holima's, too. But what about the frantic little bird? Is that how I've been acting?"

For the first time in his life, Natsama felt that he did not really know himself. "How can this be?" he moaned. "I am Natsama the great hunter." But somehow his words sounded hollow and meaningless.

Natsama returned to the ridge where he had first seen the bald eagle. Resting against an ancient cedar tree, he prayed for guidance. The determined youth waited three days and two nights, hoping for a sign that would lead him to the dreambird.

On the evening of the third day, a full moon rose over the horizon. Again the young hunter dreamed of Holima slowly stirring her fire. This time the flames transformed into a brilliant golden bird that stood as tall as he. At first Natsama was overjoyed. But when he saw the bird's wings hanging limply at its sides, a deep sense of sadness filled his heart.

21

Suddenly a huge, crimson snake appeared in the smoky shadows.
Hissing fiercely, the creature unwound its tight coils and slithered closer.
Natsama shuddered as the snake towered overhead, flicking its forked tongue
between long, sharp fangs.

The bird crouched and looked up, struggling in vain to fly away. But its wings were useless. Natsama knew the beautiful bird would soon be crushed within the snake's deadly coils. Despite his fear, the young hunter moved forward to protect the golden bird. "Let my spirit fill your wings!" he cried.   23

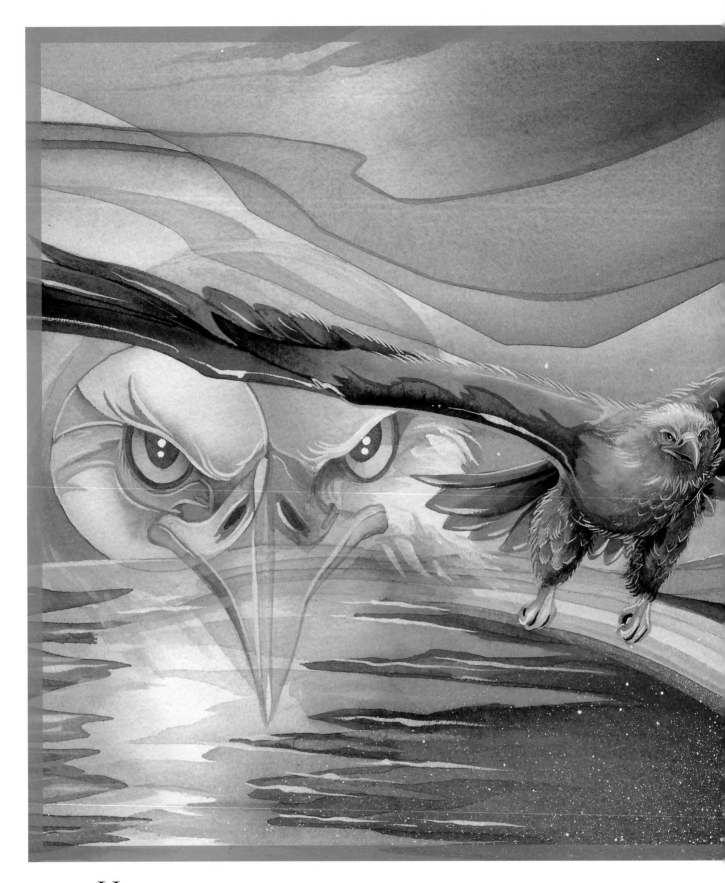

Up, up they soared, high above the Earth. On the tip of the bird's left wing was the setting moon; on the right was the rising sun. Below, a full-circle rainbow rose through the sparkling mist.

24

Off in the distance, Natsama saw Holima gliding toward him like a great white eagle. Radiant with a light brighter than the sun, the medicine woman reached out to her grandson. At that moment he heard her say, "Your true name is now Wind Warrior."

When he awoke the next morning, Natsama ran to his grandmother's lodge and stood just inside the door. Holima motioned that he should sit next to her, instead of in his customary place across the fire. Warmed by the flames, Natsama patiently waited for her to speak.

"Have you found your dreambird?" she asked softly.

"You know I have, Grandmother."

"What is your dreambird, Grandson?"

26   "It is the part of me that soars with the great eagle."

Holima smiled knowingly. "And what is your dreambird's gift?"

He paused for a moment and took a deep breath. "Embracing the power and wonder of my own spirit. That is the dreambird's gift. I'll never be the same again, Grandmother."

"You have found your true self," Holima whispered. "That which was hidden has now been revealed. You have always been Wind Warrior."

As the medicine woman smiled, Wind Warrior saw his reflection shining in her moon-pale eyes.

"The source of all things
is like a circle. It is
where everything begins
and everything returns."

DAVID OGDEN
Author

David Ogden is a licensed physical therapist and a published author in the field of aquatic therapy. *Dreambirds* is his first published children's book. This magical story was inspired by his own spiritual interests, as well as legends and myths read to him by his mother and grandmother.

At a critical point in his life, David's path crossed that of Florence Becker. Her spirit touched his soul as she helped him achieve the self-discipline essential for undertaking his spiritual journey. The next year he met Michelina Russo, who enabled him to remove obstacles created by cultural influences during childhood. In writing *Dreambirds*, he was profoundly influenced by these two wise women.

A resident of Phoenix, Arizona, David shares his house with a menagerie of exotic birds, two dogs, assorted fish, turtles, and a cat. When not writing, he is often busy vacuuming.

JODY BERGSMA
Illustrator

Jody Bergsma is an internationally acclaimed artist, known for her excellence in a wide variety of styles. In addition to creating the inspiring illustrations for *Dreambirds*, she provided invaluable creative assistance in the development of the story.

Jody's childhood was spent along the shores of a remote lake in northwest Washington State. Living near the San Juan Islands, she was greatly influenced by her bush pilot father and "very adventurous" mother. Jody believes that her creativity springs largely from the richness and beauty she experienced in her youth.

Jody's first illustrated book, *The Right Touch*, is scheduled for re-release by Illumination Arts in 1997. Her third illustrated book, *Sky Castle*, is scheduled for 1998.

In between frequent national tours, Jody lives with her husband and two children near Bellingham, Washington. Named the city's outstanding businessperson in 1995,

Jody Bergsma

Ms. Bergsma is widely appreciated for her contagious spirit of optimism. The spacious and highly successful Bergsma Gallery is a landmark in Bellingham.

In recent years, Jody has traveled extensively researching coastal tribes, their myths and art forms. Her visits to the Queen Charlotte Islands, Alaska, and the Olympic Peninsula provided much of the inspiration for these powerful illustrations.

*Dedicated to the coastal tribes and to
the Spirit of this great land.*

Author Appreciation:
With heartfelt thanks to John Thompson, Ruth Thompson, Arrieana Thompson, Judy
Tompkins, Alison McIntosh, Jody Bergsma, Molly Murrah, Gary Senter, Dorothy
Johansen, George and Frances Ogden, Hattie Taylor.

Artist Appreciation:
Special thanks to Robin Wright for her excellent and impromptu art classes
on my visit to the Queen Charlotte Islands. Without her help, I may never have
unraveled the mystery of native coastal design. Robin is the Native American Art
Curator for The Burke Museum in Seattle, Washington.

First edition published by

ILLUMINATION ARTS
PUBLISHING COMPANY, INC.

P.O. BOX 1865

BELLEVUE, WA 98009

TEL: 425-646-3670

Library of Congress Cataloging-in-Publication Data

Ogden, David, 1941 -

Dreambirds / written by David Ogden; illustrated by Jody Bergsma.

p. cm.

Summary: A young Native American boy spends his youth searching for the dreambird his grandmother has told him will reveal his special gift.

ISBN: 0-935699-09-0 $16.95

1. Indians of North America – Juvenile Fiction. [1. Indians of North America– Fiction. 2. Grandmothers–Fiction.]

I. Bergsma, Jody, ill., 1955- II. Title.

PZ7.0334Dr 1997

[Fic]–dc21

Published in the United States of America

Printed by Tien Wah Press of Singapore

Book Designer:

Molly Murrah, Murrah & Company, Kirkland, WA

These special children's books are available at fine bookstores everywhere.

DREAMBIRDS

by David Ogden $16.95

The magical story of a young Native American boy's search for the elusive dreambird.

CORNELIUS AND THE DOGSTAR

by Diana Spyropulos $15.95

Cornelius, a grouchy old basset hound, is turned away at the gates of Dog Heaven. During his amazing journey of self-discovery, he learns about generosity, kindness, playfulness and love.

ALL I SEE IS PART OF ME

by Chara M. Curtis $15.95

Through a series of illuminating experiences, a young child explores his world and awakens to his connection with all of life. An international bestseller.

FUN IS A FEELING

by Chara M. Curtis $14.95

In this poetic journey, a child discovers the wonder of his imagination and learns to see the fun hidden in everyday life.

HOW FAR TO HEAVEN?

by Chara M. Curtis $15.95

During an enchanting walk through the woods, Nanna helps her granddaughter to see the signs of heaven in all of nature.

Direct Orders: For shipping and handling add $2.00 for the first book and $1.00 for each additional book. Washington residents, please add 8.2% sales tax. VISA and Mastercard accepted.

ILLUMINATION ARTS
PUBLISHING COMPANY, INC.
P.O. BOX 1865
BELLEVUE, WA 98009
TEL: 425-646-3670
FAX: 425-646-4144
1-888-210-8216

Jody Bergsma's limited edition prints and cards are available through the Bergsma Gallery in Bellingham, Washington at 1-800-BERGSMA (1-800-237-4762).